This Boxer Books paperback
belongs to

....

To Oscar and Leo
S.B.

First published in hardback in the UK in 2018 by Boxer Books Limited.

This paperback edition published in 2019.

www.boxerbooks.com

Boxer® is a registered trademark of Boxer Books Limited

Text and illustrations copyright © 2018 Sebastien Braun

The rights of Sebastien Braun to be identified as the author and illustrator of this work
have been asserted by him in accordance with the Copyright, Designs and Patents Act. 1988.

The illustrations were prepared in mixed media.

A catalogue record of this book is available from the British Library.

ISBN 978-1-910716-83-0

10 9 8 7 6 5 4 3 2 1

Printed in China

All of our papers are sourced from managed forests and renewable resources.

I Love My
BABY

Sebastien Braun

Boxer Books

I kiss my baby
every morning.

I give my babies
food to eat.

I bring my babies
sweet surprises.

I love to take
my baby sailing.

I teach my babies
to swim at the pond.

When it rains
I like taking
long naps
with my baby.

I love it when my
babies run to me.

I watch
my baby
play in
the woods.

I keep my baby
cosy and warm.

I love to
sing songs
with
my baby.

I give my baby
big snuggly hugs.

I love my baby.

MORE BOXER BOOKS BY SEBASTIEN BRAUN

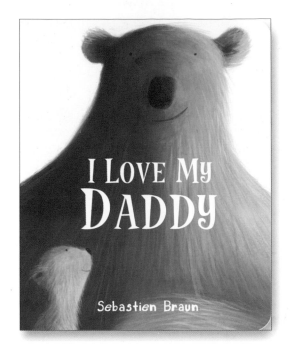

'I defy any parent to put this book back on the shelf after picking it up.'
THE BOOKSELLER

'Sumptuous illustrations... Soft colours evoke the woodland setting, creating a perfect backdrop to this sensitive tale.'
JUNIOR MAGAZINE

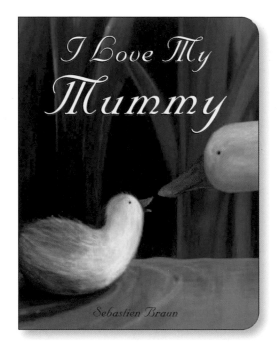

'Beautifully produced with some charming and warmly coloured illustrations.'
MONTESSORI INTERNATIONAL

SHORTLISTED IN THE BOOKTRUST EARLY YEARS AWARDS 2006

'With unadorned, heartfelt prose and idyllic images, Braun conveys how wonderful it feels to spend a day alone with Daddy.'
PUBLISHERS WEEKLY

'Each measured word builds the gentle narrative; the sweet conclusion perfectly complements the quiet tale... The consistently child-centered voice provides a lovely depiction of the journey home and those priceless moments shared by a father and his child.'
SCHOOL LIBRARY JOURNAL